CLEOPATRA BONES

AND THE
GOLDEN CHIMPANZEE

Cleopatra Bones

Al McNasty

Ringo and Ramona
Lamarr

Jumping Jack O'Malley

Leo
Longclaw

Diego Del
Grippo

Ella Egghart

Jango Karbunkel

CLEOPATRA BONES

AND THE GOLDEN CHIMPANZEE

I've cracked the code! C.B.

Jonathan Emmett

Ed Eaves

Kane Miller
A DIVISION OF EDC PUBLISHING

In the ruins of a temple,
down a dark and winding stair,
explorer Cleopatra Bones is
creeping with great care.

Springing nimbly sideways
to avoid a deadly trap . . .

... she squeezes through a
secret door and finds
a TREASURE MAP!

Back at the museum,
the experts all agree,
the map shows the location of
THE GOLDEN CHIMPANZEE.

A priceless, precious statue, or so the stories say,
but no one knew its whereabouts—at least until today.

The Chimpanzee is hidden in the Jungle of Junoo,
in the Vakamamma Valley on the shore of Lake Lazoo.

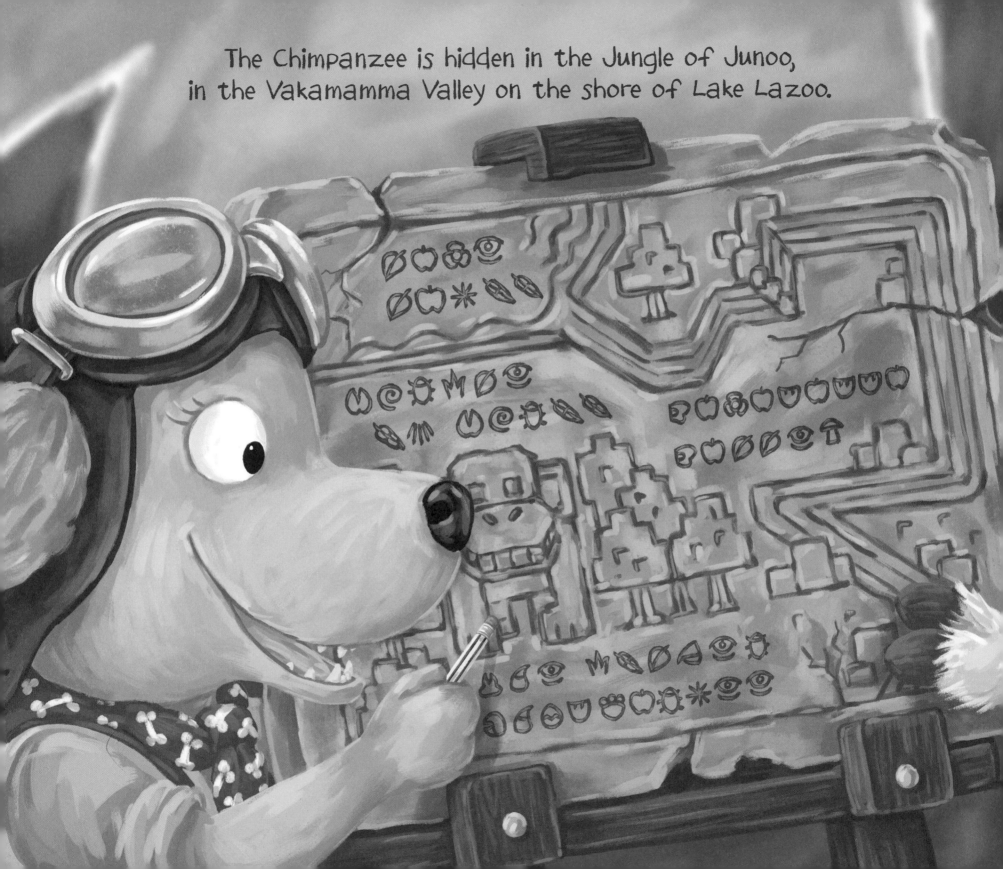

Everyone's excited that the secret's out at last.

But the news is spreading quickly, so they'd better get there FAST.

Speeding up the river, the first to reach the valley
is the famous frog adventurer Jumping Jack O'Malley.

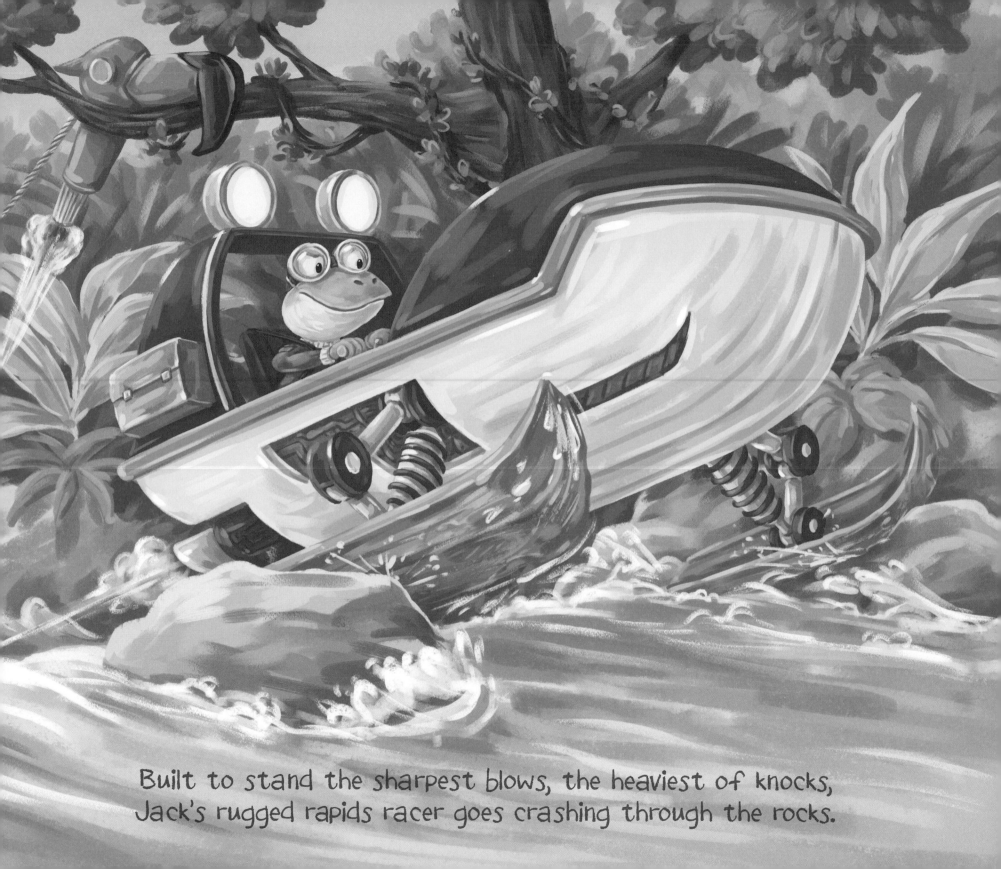

Built to stand the sharpest blows, the heaviest of knocks,
Jack's rugged rapids racer goes crashing through the rocks.

Next, the valley echoes with a noisy whirring sound
as Leo Longclaw's jungle copter lowers to the ground.

Before the copter's landed,
Leo's bounded out the door,
and plunged into the jungle
with a treasure-hungry roar.

Cleopatra Bones arrives by powered parachute. The others see her circling round and set off in pursuit.

Something on the ground below has clearly caught her eye.
And whatever she is heading for, they want to be nearby.

It's a massive monkey statue, overlooked and overgrown.
It's certainly a chimpanzee, but this one's made of STONE.

So the quest continues, but the searchers don't go far,
before they're interrupted by . . .

. . . an armored aqua car!

The aqua car skids to a stop beside the statue's feet.
And out springs Al McNasty, that greedy, grasping cheat!

Al's sure he knows just where the missing treasure can be found.
He's certain that the Chimpanzee is buried underground.

But Al is much too lazy
to go digging with a spade.
Why dig a hole by hand when
there's a fortune to be made?

And it would take forever, why he might be there all night.
So Al's going to BLAST A HOLE with sticks of DYNAMITE!

The valley echoes as this awful alligator
pushes down the plunger and creates a massive crater.
There's lots of dirt and rubble, but to Al's immense displeasure,
there's no sign of the Golden Chimp or any other treasure!

The blast wave shook the valley
and behind Al's scaly back,
the ancient statue splits apart
with an almighty crack.

And then, before McNasty has the time to turn around, the statue's bottom falls on him and pins him to the ground.

And from the broken body pours a waterfall of gold,
a glittering, glistening torrent that's a wonder to behold.

It seems that this stone statue WAS the treasure that they sought.
But it's golden on the INSIDE, not the outside as they'd thought.

There's gold enough for everyone to have an ample share,
so Cleopatra and the others split it, fair and square.

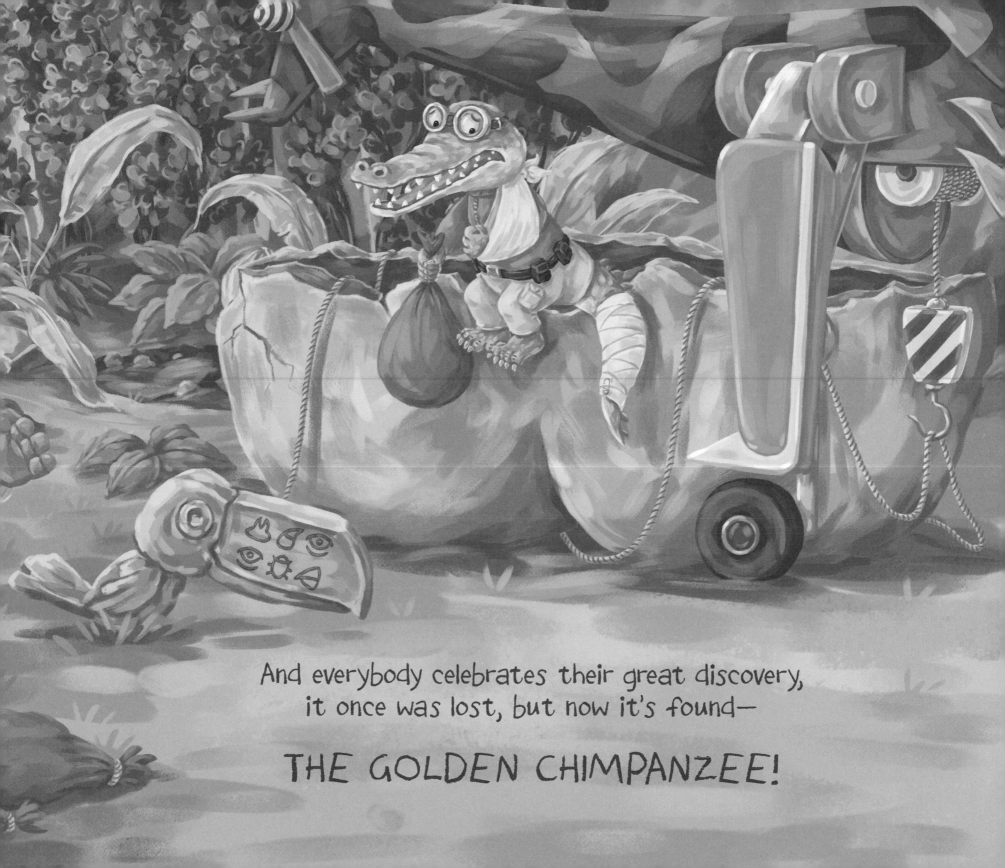

And everybody celebrates their great discovery,
it once was lost, but now it's found—

THE GOLDEN CHIMPANZEE!

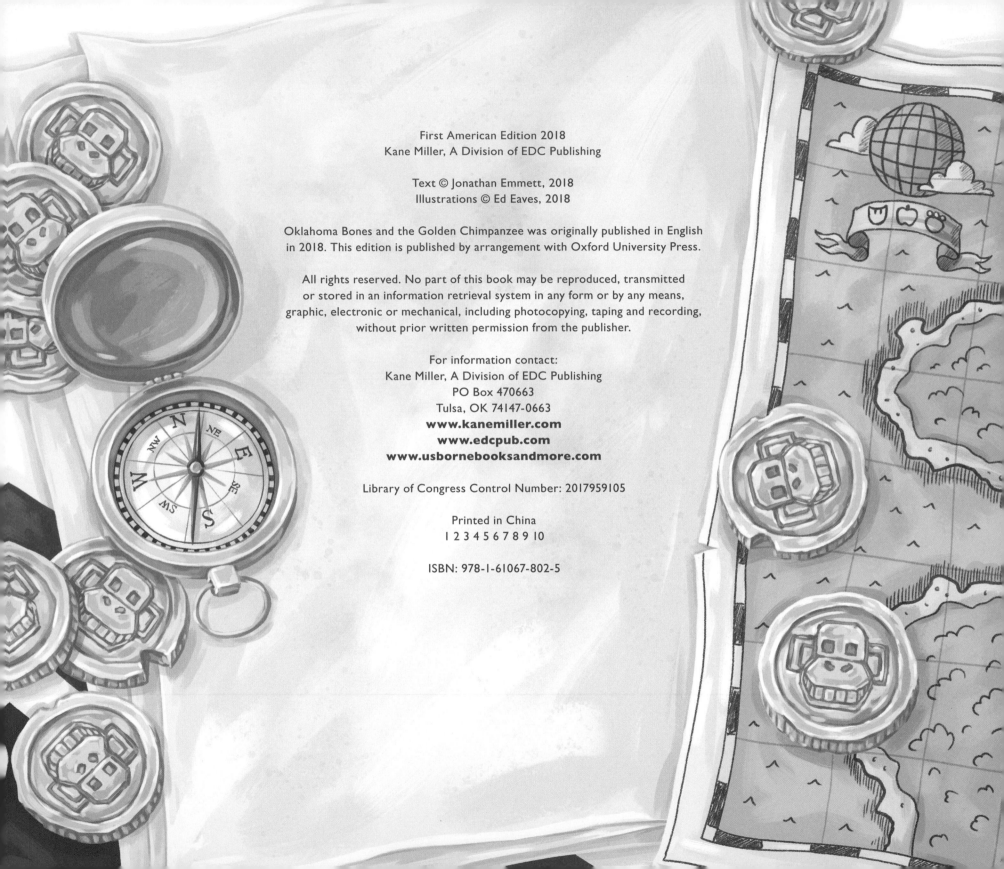

First American Edition 2018
Kane Miller, A Division of EDC Publishing

Text © Jonathan Emmett, 2018
Illustrations © Ed Eaves, 2018

Oklahoma Bones and the Golden Chimpanzee was originally published in English
in 2018. This edition is published by arrangement with Oxford University Press.

For information contact:
Kane Miller, A Division of EDC Publishing
PO Box 470663
Tulsa, OK 74147-0663
www.kanemiller.com
www.edcpub.com
www.usbornebooksandmore.com

Library of Congress Control Number: 2017959105

Printed in China
1 2 3 4 5 6 7 8 9 10

ISBN: 978-1-61067-802-5

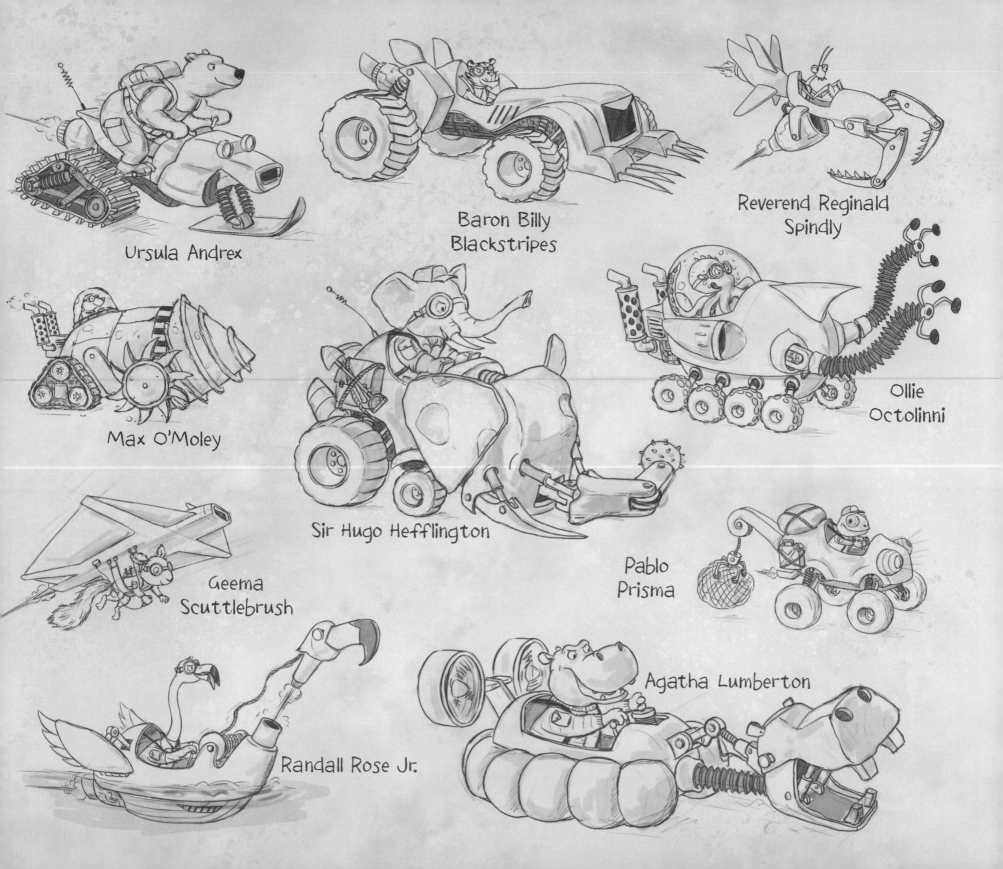

Ursula Andrex

Baron Billy
Blackstripes

Reverend Reginald
Spindly

Max O'Moley

Sir Hugo Hefflington

Ollie
Octolinni

Geema
Scuttlebrush

Pablo
Prisma

Randall Rose Jr.

Agatha Lumberton